MARK
TWAIN

THE DIARIES OF EVE & ADAM

ADAPTED BY:
JEROME TILLER
ILLUSTRATED BY:
MARC JOHNSON-PENCOOK

The Diaries of Eve and Adam
Second Edition- Revised and Expanded
By Mark Twain
Adapted by Jerome Tiller
Illustrated by Marc Johnson-Pencook

ISBN 978-1-939846-34-1

Produced and Published by ArtWrite Productions

artwriteproductions.com

Publishing Imprint - Adapted Classics

adaptedclassics.com

Cover Design: Kristina Brown
kristinadesignz.com

PREFACE

This is an adaptation of two separate stories that I combined into one. The original stories were written by Mark Twain, one of the world's all-time greatest authors. To combine the stories we omitted some passages, relocated many, and added some new material. Other changes (paragraph breaks, minor rearrangements, minor additions and omissions, etc.) were made to accommodate the illustration of characters and critical scenes in the story. Some changes (word choice, word order, etc.) were made to expand its accessibility and appeal, keeping modern youth in mind. No change was made with the notion it would improve the text or the stories in any way.

The original stories are classics—please make a point to read them sooner or later. You are bound to enjoy them when you do!

Among other places, the original versions of Extracts from Adam's Diary and Eve's Diary can be found at:

http://www.gutenberg.org/

EVE'S FIRST SATURDAY. – I am almost a whole day old now. I arrived yesterday. That is as it seems to me. And it must be so, for if there was a day-before-yesterday, I was not there when it happened or I should remember it. It could be, of course, that it did happen, and that I was not noticing. Very well; I will be very watchful now, and if any day-before-yesterdays happen I will make a note of it. It will be best to start right and not let the record get confused, for some instinct tells me that these details are going to be important to the historian some day.

This majestic new world is indeed a most noble and beautiful work and certainly marvelously near to being perfect. Look at the moon! There isn't another thing among the ornaments and decorations that is comparable to the moon for beauty and finish. Stars are good, too. There are too many stars in some places and not enough in others, but that can be remedied presently, no doubt.

I wish I could get some to put in my hair. I tried to knock some down with a pole, but it didn't reach, which astonished me. Then I tried clods till I was all tired out, but I never got one. I thought it was because I am left-handed and could not throw good enough. But I suppose I never can get a star down. You would be surprised to find how far off they are, for they do not look it.

I feel like an experiment, exactly like an experiment. It would be impossible for a person to feel more like an experiment than I do, and so I am coming to feel convinced that is what I AM - an experiment; just an experiment, and nothing more. Then if I am an experiment, am I the whole of it? No, I think not. I think the rest of it—the other—is part of the experiment. I am the main part of it, but I think the rest of it has its share in the matter. Is my position assured, or do I have to watch my position and take care of it? The latter, perhaps.

Some instinct tells me that eternal vigilance is the price of supremacy. (That is a good phrase, I think, for one so young.)

EVE'S MONDAY. – I followed the other Experiment around yesterday afternoon at a distance to see what it might be for, if I could. But I was not able to make that out. I realize that I feel more curiosity about it than about any of the other reptiles. If it is a reptile, and I suppose it is, for it has frowzy hair and blue eyes and it looks like a reptile. It has no hips; it tapers like a carrot. And when it stands it spreads itself apart like a derrick. So I think it is a reptile, though it may be architecture. I was afraid of it at first and started to run every time it turned around, for I thought it was going to chase me. But by and by I found it was only trying to get away. After realizing that, I was not timid any more. So I tracked it along, several hours, about twenty yards behind, which made it nervous and unhappy. At last it was a good deal worried, and climbed a tree. I waited a good while at the tree, then gave it up and went home.

ADAM'S MONDAY. – This new creature with the long hair is a good deal in the way. It is always hanging around and following me about. I don't like this. I am not used to company. I wish it would stay with the other animals.

EVE'S TUESDAY. – Today the same thing over. I've got it up the tree again.

EVE'S FRIDAY. – Wednesday, Thursday, and today, all without seeing it. It is a long time to be alone. Still, it is better to be alone than unwelcome. I had to have company—I was made for it, I think. So I made friends with the animals. They are just charming, and they have the kindest disposition and the politest ways. They never look sour, never let you feel that you are intruding. They smile at you and wag their tail—if they've got one—and they are always ready for a romp or an excursion or anything you want to propose.

The birds and animals are all friendly to each other, and there are no disputes about anything. They all talk, and they all talk to me. But it must be a foreign language, for I cannot make out a word they say. Yet they often understand me when I talk back, particularly the dog and the elephant. It shows that they are brighter than I am. It makes me ashamed, for I want to be the principal Experiment myself, and I intend to be, too.

All these days we have had such good times, and it hasn't been lonesome for me, ever. Lonesome! No, I should say not. Why, there's always a swarm of them around—sometimes as much as four or five acres. You can't count them. And when you stand on a rock in the midst and look out over the furry expanse, it is so mottled and splashed and gay with color and frisking sheen and sun-flash, and so rippled with stripes, that you might think it was a lake, only you know it isn't. And there's storms of sociable birds, and hurricanes of whirring wings. When the sun strikes all that feathery commotion, you have a blazing up of all the colors you can think of, enough to put your eyes out.

We have made long excursions, and I have seen a great deal of the world. Almost all of it, I think. So I am the first traveler, and the only one. When we are on the march, it is an imposing sight. There's nothing like it anywhere. For comfort I ride a tiger or a leopard, because both are soft and have a round back that fits me, and also because they are such pretty animals. But for long distance or for scenery, I ride the elephant. It hoists me up with his trunk, but I can get off myself; when we are ready to camp, it sits and I slide down the back way.

EVE'S SECOND SATURDAY. – It is up there yet. Resting, apparently. But that is a subterfuge: Saturday isn't the day of rest; Sunday is appointed for that. It looks to me like a creature that is more interested in resting than in anything else. It would tire me to rest so much. It tires me just to sit around and watch the tree. I do wonder what it is for; I never see it do anything worthwhile.

But I have seen it has low tastes and is not kind. When I went there yesterday evening in the gloaming, it had crept down and was trying to catch the little speckled fishes that play in the pool. I had to clod it to make it go up the tree again and let them alone. I wonder if *that* is what it is for? Hasn't it any heart? Hasn't it any compassion for those little creatures? Can it be that it was designed and manufactured for such ungentle work? It has the look of it. One of the clods took up hard to the back of its ear, and it used language. That gave me a thrill, for it was the first time I had ever heard speech, except my own. I did not understand the words, but they seemed expressive.

When I found it could talk I felt a new interest in it, for I love to talk. I talk all day, and in my sleep, too, and I am very interesting. But if I had another to talk to I could be twice as interesting, and I would never stop, if desired.

I think it is a man. I had never seen a man, but it looked like one, and I feel sure that is what it is. If this reptile is a man, it isn't an *it*, is it? I think it would be *he*. I think so. In that case, I will consider it a man and call it 'he' until it turns out to be something else. This will be handier than having so many uncertainties.

ADAM. – The new creature says its name is Eve. That is all right—I have no objections. Says Eve is what to call it by when I want it to come. When I want it to come? I said her name was superfluous then. The word 'superfluous' evidently raised me in its respect; and indeed it is a large, good word and will bear repetition. It also says it is not an *it*, it is a *she*. This is probably doubtful, yet it is all one to me. What she is were nothing to me if she would but go by herself and not talk. She told me she was made out of a rib taken from my body. This is at least doubtful, if not more than that. I have not missed any rib.

Built me a shelter, but could not have it to myself in peace. The new creature intruded. When I tried to put it out, it shed water out of the holes it looks with, and wiped it away with the back of its paws, and made a noise such as some of the other animals make when they are in distress.

EVE. – This morning I told him my name, hoping it would interest him. But he did not care for it. Although he talks so little, he has quite a considerable vocabulary. He used a surprisingly good word this morning. He evidently recognized himself that it was a good one, for he worked it into comments twice afterward, casually. That was good conversational art, which goes to show that he possesses a certain quality of perception. Without a doubt that seed can be made to grow, if cultivated. Where did he get that word? I do not think I have ever used it.

It is strange. If he should tell me his name, I would care. I think it would be pleasanter in my ears than any other sound. But he took no interest in my name. I tried to hide my disappointment, but I suppose I did not succeed. I went away sad and sat on the moss-bank with my feet in the water. It is where I go when I hunger for companionship—someone to look at, someone to talk to. It is not enough, that lovely white body painted there in the pool. But it is something, and something is better than utter loneliness. It talks when I talk; it is sad when I am sad; it comforts me with its sympathy. It says, "Do not be downhearted, you poor friendless girl. *I* will be your friend". It *is* a good friend to me, and my only one; it is my sister. Many and many are the visits I have paid her. She is my comfort and my refuge when my life is hard—and it is mainly that.

ADAM. – She fell in the pond yesterday when she was looking at herself in it, which she is always doing. She nearly strangled. She said that felt most uncomfortable, which made her sorry for the creatures that live in the pond, which she calls fish. For she continues to fasten names onto things that don't need them and that don't come when they are called by them, which is a matter of no consequence to her. She is such a numb-skull. Anyway, so she got a lot of them so-called fish out of the pond and brought them in last night and put them in my bed to keep warm. I don't see that made them any happier than they were before, only quieter. When night comes I shall throw them outdoors. I will not sleep with them again. I find them clammy and unpleasant to lie among when a person hasn't anything on.

EVE. – All the week I tagged around after him and tried to get acquainted. I had to do the talking because he was shy, but I didn't mind it. He seemed pleased to have me around. I used the sociable "we" a good deal because it seemed to flatter him to be included.

ADAM. –Cloudy today, wind in the east; think we shall have rain. *We?* Where did I get that word?... I remember now—the new creature uses it.

EVE. – He talks so very little. Perhaps it is because he is not bright and is sensitive about it and wishes to conceal it. It is such a pity that he should feel so, for brightness is nothing. It is in the heart that the values lie. I wish I could make him understand that a loving, good heart is riches, and riches enough, and that without heart, intellect is poverty.

ADAM. – I wish it would not talk; it is always talking. That sounds like a cheap fling, a slur at the poor creature. But I do not mean it so. I have never heard the human voice before, and any new and strange sound intruding itself here upon the solemn hush of these dreaming solitudes offends my ear and seems a false note. And this new sound is so close to me—right at my shoulder, right at my ear, first on one side and then on the other. I am used only to sounds that are more or less distant from me.

EVE. – All the morning I was at work improving the estate; and I purposely kept away from him in the hope that he would get lonely and come. But he did not. At noon I stopped for the day and took my recreation by flitting all about with the bees and the butterflies and reveling in the flowers, those beautiful creatures that catch the smile of God out of the sky and preserve it! I gathered them, and made them into wreaths and garlands and clothed myself in them while I ate my luncheon—apples, of course. Then I sat in the shade and wished and waited. But he did not come.

No matter. Nothing would have come of it, for he does not care for flowers. He called them rubbish and cannot tell one from another. He thinks it is superior to feel like that. He does not care for me, he does not care for flowers, he does not care for the painted sky at eventide. Is there anything he does care for, except building shacks to coop himself up in from the good clean rain, and thumping the melons, and sampling the grapes, and fingering the fruit on the trees to see how those properties are coming along?

ADAM. – *We* again—that is *its* word. Mine, too, now, from hearing it so much. Good deal of fog this morning. I do not go out in the fog myself. This new creature does. It goes out in all weathers, and stumps right in with its muddy feet. And talks. It used to be so pleasant and quiet here.

Perhaps I ought to remember that she is very young, a mere girl, and make allowances. She is all interest, eagerness, vivacity. The world is to her a charm, a wonder, a mystery, a joy. She cannot speak for the delight she feels when she finds a new flower; she must pet it and caress it and smell it and talk to it and pour out endearing names upon it. And she is color-mad: brown rocks, yellow sand, gray moss, green foliage, blue sky, the pearl of the dawn, the purple shadows on the mountains, the golden islands floating in crimson seas at sunset, the pallid moon sailing through the shredded cloud-rack, the star-jewels glittering in the wastes of space. None of them is of any practical value, so far as I can see, but because they have color and majesty, that is enough for her, and she loses her mind over them.

If she could quiet down and keep still a couple minutes at a time, that would be a reposeful spectacle. And if that were to happen I think I could enjoy looking at her. Indeed, I am sure I could, for I am coming to realize that she is a quite remarkably comely creature—lithe, slender, trim, rounded, shapely, nimble, graceful. And once when she was standing marble-white and sun-drenched on a boulder, with her young head tilted back and her hand shading her eyes watching the flight of a bird in the sky, I recognized that she was beautiful.

EVE. – We are getting along very well indeed, now, and getting better and better acquainted. He does not try to avoid me any more, which is a good sign, and shows that he likes to have me with him. That pleases me. I study to be useful to him in every way I can, so as to increase his regard. During the last day or two I have taken all the work of naming things off his hands, and this has been a great relief to him. He has no gift in that line, and is evidently very grateful. He can't think of a rational name to save him, but I do not let him see that I am aware of his defect. Whenever a new creature comes along, I name it before he has time to expose himself by an awkward silence. In this way I have saved him many embarrassments. I have no defect like this. The minute I set eyes on an animal, I know what it is. I don't have to reflect a moment; the right name comes out instantly, just as if it were an inspiration. As no doubt it is, for I am sure it wasn't in me half a minute before. I seem to know just by the shape of the creature and the way it acts what animal it is.

ADAM. – Been examining the great waterfall. It is the finest thing on the estate, I think. The new creature calls it Niagara Falls. Why? I am sure I do not know. Says it *looks* like Niagara Falls. This naming goes recklessly on, in spite of anything I can do. I had a very good name for the estate, and it was musical and pretty—GARDEN OF EDEN.

GOAT ISLE
WHIRLPOOL
KEEP OFF
CAVE OF THE WINDS
NIAGARA FALLS PARK

Privately, I continue to call it that, but not any longer publicly. The new creature says it is all woods and rocks and scenery, and therefore has no resemblance to a garden. Says it *looks* like a park, and does not look like anything *but* a park. That is not a reason. It is mere waywardness and imbecility. Consequently, without consulting me, the estate has been new-named NIAGARA FALLS PARK. This is sufficiently high-handed, it seems to me. I get no chance to name anything myself. And already there is a sign up: KEEP OFF THE GRASS. She has littered the whole estate with very bad names and offensive signs: This way to the Whirlpool—This way to Goat Island—Cave of the Winds this way. She says this park would make a tidy summer resort if there was any custom for it. Summer resort—another invention of hers. Just words, without any meaning. What is a summer resort? But it is best not to ask her. She has such a rage for explaining. My life is not as happy as it was.

EVE. – When the dodo came along he thought it was a wildcat. I saw it in his eye. But I saved him. And I was careful not to do it in a way that could hurt his pride. I just spoke up in a quite natural way of pleasing surprise, and not as if I was dreaming of conveying information. I said, "Well, I do declare, if there isn't the dodo!" I explained—without seeming to be explaining—how I know it for a dodo. And although I thought maybe he was a little wounded that I knew the creature when he didn't, it was quite evident that he admired me. That was very agreeable, and I thought of it more than once with gratification before I slept. How little a thing can make us happy when we feel that we have earned it!

ADAM. – The new creature names everything that comes along before I can get in a protest. And always that same pretext is offered—it *looks* like the thing. There is a dodo, for instance. Says the moment one looks at it one sees at a glance that it "looks like a dodo". It will have to keep that name, no doubt. It wearies me to fret about it, and it does no good, anyway. Dodo! It looks no more like a dodo than I do.

She has taken to beseeching me to stop going over the Falls. What harm does it do? Says it makes her shudder. I wonder why; I have always done it—always liked the plunge, and coolness. I supposed it was what the Falls were for. They have no other use that I can see, and they must have been made for something. She says they were only made for scenery—like the rhinoceros and the mastodon.

I went over the Falls in a barrel—not satisfactory to her. Went over in a tub—still not satisfactory. Swam the Whirlpool and the Rapids in a fig-leaf suit. It got much damaged. Hence, tedious complaints about my extravagance. I am too much hampered here. I need a change of scene. I will escape and build me another shelter in a secluded place, and obliterate my tracks as well as I can.

EVE. – My first sorrow. Yesterday he avoided me and seemed to wish I would not talk to him. I could not believe it, and thought there was some mistake, for I loved to be with him, and loved to hear him talk. So how could it be that he could feel unkind toward me when I had not done anything? But he put me out in the rain, and it was my first sorrow. So I went away and sat lonely in the place where I first saw him the morning that we were made, and when I did not know what he was and was indifferent about him. But now it was a mournful place. And every little think in my head spoke of him, and my heart was very sore. I did not know why very clearly for it was a new feeling. I had not experienced it before, and it was all a mystery. I could not make it out. But after two days I could not bear the lonesomeness. I went to the new shelter which he has built to ask him what I had done that was wrong and how I could mend it and get back his kindness again.

ADAM. – She hunted me out by means of a beast which she has tamed and calls a wolf, and came making that pitiful noise again, and shedding that water out of the places she looks with. I was obliged to return with her, but will presently emigrate again when occasion offers.

EVE. – It is pleasant again, now, and I am happy. But those were heavy days. I do not think of them when I can help it.

ADAM. – If there is anything on the planet that she is not interested in it is not in my list. There are animals that I am indifferent to, but it is not so with her. She has no discrimination. She takes to all of them! She thinks they are all treasures! Every new one is welcome!

When the mighty brontosaurus came striding into camp, she regarded it as an acquisition. I considered it a calamity. That is a good sample of the lack of harmony that prevails in our views of things. She wanted to domesticate it—I wanted to make it a present of the homestead and move out. She believed it could be tamed by kind treatment and would be a good pet—I said a pet twenty-one feet high and eighty-four feet long would be no proper thing to have about the place! Because even with the best intentions and without meaning any harm, it could sit down on the house and mash it! Anyone could see by the look of its eye that it was absent-minded.

Still, her heart was set upon having that monster and she couldn't give it up. She thought we could start a dairy with it, and wanted me to help milk it. But I wouldn't! It was too risky. We hadn't any ladder, and the sex wasn't right anyway! Then she wanted to ride it and look at the scenery. Thirty or forty feet of its tail was lying on the ground, like a fallen tree, and she thought she could climb it. But she was mistaken. When she got to the steep place it was too slick and down she came. She would have hurt herself but for me.

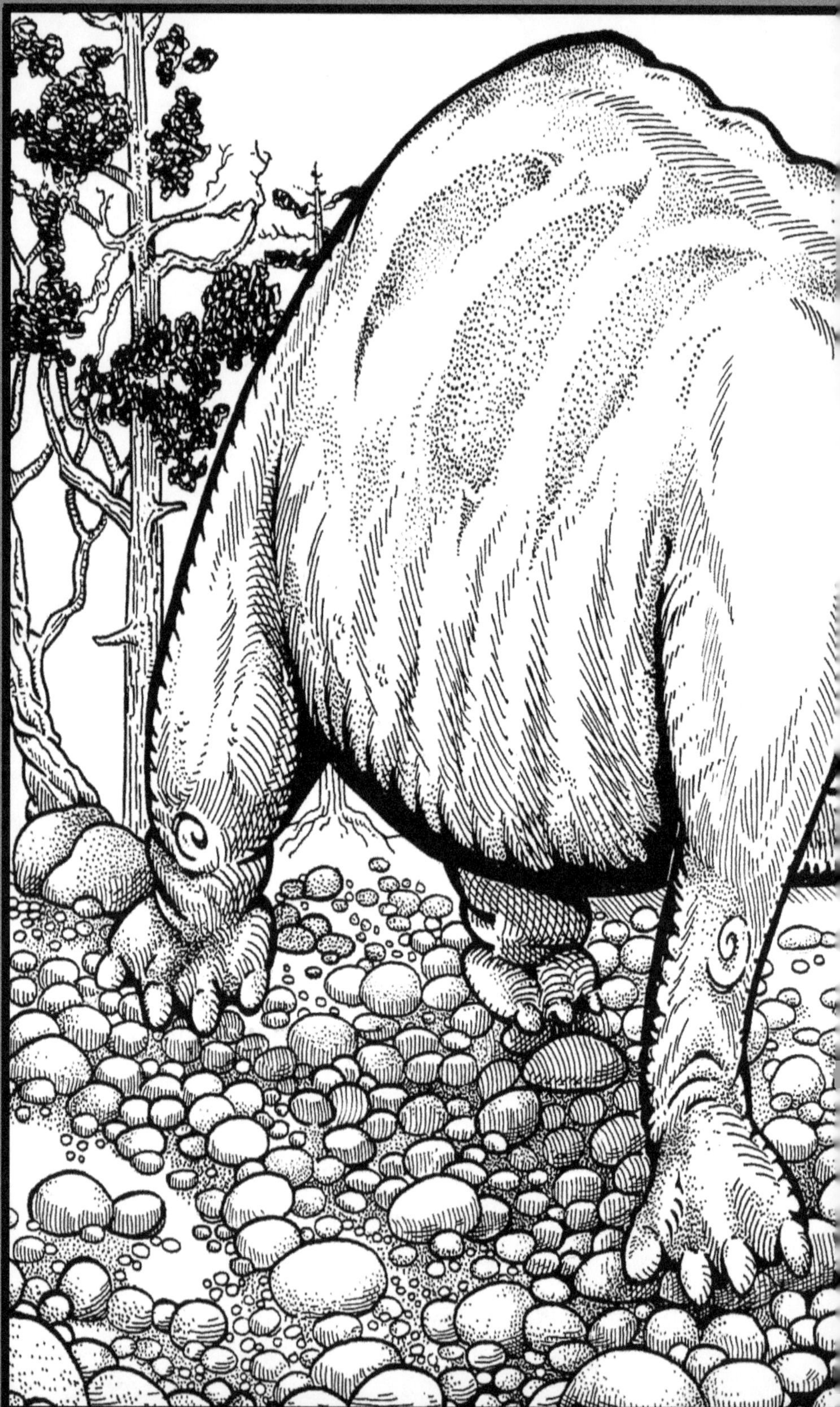

But was she satisfied now? No. Nothing ever satisfies her but demonstration. Untested theories are not in her line, and she won't have them. I concede she has the right spirit and I concede it attracts me. I feel the influence of it. If I were with her more I think I should take it up myself. Well, she had one theory remaining about this colossus brontosaurus: she thought that if we could tame it and make him friendly we could stand it in the river and use him for a bridge. It turned out that he was already plenty tame enough—at least as far as she was concerned—so she tried her theory, but it failed. Every time she got him properly placed in the river and went ashore to cross over him, he came out and followed her around like a pet mountain. Just like the other animals! They all do that!

EVE. – I have learned a number of things and am educated now, but I wasn't at first. I was ignorant at first. At first it used to vex me because, with all my watching, I was never smart enough to be around when the water was running uphill. But now I do not mind it. I have experimented and experimented until now I know it never does run uphill, except in the dark. I know it does in the dark, because the pool never goes dry, which it would, of course, if the water didn't come back in the night.

It is best to prove things by actual experiment; then you *know*. Whereas if you depend on guessing and supposing and conjecturing, you never get educated. Some things you *can't* find out; but you will never know you can't by guessing and supposing. No, you have to be patient and go on experimenting until you find out that you can't find out.

And it is delightful to have it that way—it makes the world so interesting. If there wasn't anything to find out, it would be dull. Even trying to find out and not finding out is just as interesting as trying to find out and finding out, and I don't know if not *more* so. The secret of the water flow was a treasure until I *got* it. Then the excitement all went away and I recognized a sense of loss.

ADAM. – She engages herself in many foolish things. Among others, she studies to find out why the animals called lions and tigers live on grass and flowers when, as she says, the sort of teeth they wear would indicate that they were intended to eat each other. This is foolish because to do that would be to kill each other. And that would introduce what, as I understand, is called "death".And death, as I have been told, has not yet entered the Park. Which is a pity, on some accounts. She is in much trouble about the buzzard. She says grass does not agree with it. She is afraid she can't raise it on grass—she thinks it was intended to live on decayed flesh. I say he buzzard must get along the best it can with what is provided. We cannot overturn the whole scheme to accommodate the buzzard!

EVE. – By experiment I know that wood swims, and dry leaves, and feathers, and plenty of other things. Therefore by all that cumulative evidence you know that a rock will swim. But you have to put up with simply knowing it for there isn't any way to prove it—up to now. I shall find a way—but then *that* excitement will go. Such things make me sad, because by and by when I have found out everything there won't be any more excitements, and I do love excitements so! The other night I couldn't sleep for thinking about it.

I think there are many things to learn yet—I hope so! And by economizing and not hurrying too fast I think they will last weeks and weeks. I hope so. When you cast up a feather it sails away on the air and goes out of sight. Then you throw up a clod and it doesn't. It comes down, every time. I have tried it and tried it, and it is always so. I wonder why it is? Of course it *doesn't* come down, but why should it *seem* to? I suppose it is an optical illusion. I mean, one of them is. I don't know which one. It may be the feather, it may be the clod; I can't prove which it is. I can only demonstrate that one or the other is a fake, and let a person take his choice.

ADAM. – The new creature eats too much fruit. We are going to run short, most likely. This morning I found the new creature trying to clod apples out of that forbidden tree. I told her she shouldn't—she will come to harm if she keeps that up.

EVE. – I tried to get him some of those apples, but I cannot learn to throw straight. I failed, but I think the good intention pleased him. They are forbidden, and he says I shall come to harm. But if I come to harm through pleasing him, why shall I care for that harm?

ADAM. – She is climbing that tree now. Clodded her out of it. She said nobody was looking. Seems to consider that sufficient justification for chancing any dangerous thing. Told her that. The word justification moved her admiration—and envy, too, I thought. It is a good word.

EVE. – At first I couldn't make out what I was made for, but now I think it was to search out the secrets of this wonderful world and be happy and thank the Giver of it all for devising it. By watching, I know that the stars are not going to last. I have seen some of the best ones melt and run down the sky. Since one can melt, they can all melt; since they can all melt, they can all melt the same night. That sorrow will come—I know it. I mean to sit up every night and look at them as long as I can keep awake; and I will impress those sparkling fields on my memory, so that by and by when they are taken away I can by my fancy restore those lovely myriads to the black sky and make them sparkle again, and double them by the blur of my tears.

ADAM. – She has taken up with a snake now. The other animals are glad, for she was always experimenting with them and bothering them. I am glad because the snake talks and this enables me to get a rest.

EVE. – I laid a dry stick on the ground and tried to bore a hole in it with another one in order to carry out a scheme that I had, but soon I got an awful fright. A thin, transparent bluish film rose out of the hole, and I dropped everything and ran! I thought it was a spirit, and I was so frightened! But I looked back, and it was not coming. So I leaned against a rock and rested and panted and let my limbs go on trembling until they got steady again. Then I crept warily back, alert, watching, and ready to fly if there was occasion. And when I was come near it again, I parted the branches of a rose-bush and peeped through—wishing the man was about to see me, I was looking so cunning and pretty. But the sprite was gone. I went there, and there was a pinch of delicate pink dust in the hole. I put my finger in, to feel it, said OUCH!—then took it out again. It was a cruel pain.

I put my finger in my mouth and, by standing first on one foot and then the other and grunting, I presently eased my misery. Then I was full of interest and began to examine.

I was curious to know what the pink dust was. Suddenly the name of it occurred to me, though I had never heard of it before. It was FIRE! I was as certain of it as a person could be of anything in the world. So without hesitation I named it that—fire.

I had created something that didn't exist before—I had added a new thing to the world's uncountable properties. I realized this and was proud of my achievement. I was going to run and find him and tell him about it, thinking to raise myself in his esteem. But I reflected and did not do it. No—he would not care for it. He would ask what it was good for, and what could I answer? For if it was not *good* for something, but only beautiful, merely beautiful, then? So I sighed and did not go, for it wasn't good for anything. It could not build a shack, it could not improve melons, it could not hurry a fruit crop. It was useless, a foolishness, a vanity. He would despise it and say cutting words. But to me it was not despicable. I said, "Oh, you fire, I love you, you dainty pink creature, for you are *beautiful*—and that is enough!" I was going to gather it to my breast, but I refrained. Then I made a maxim out of my head: "THE BURNT EXPERIMENT SHUNS THE FIRE."

I pinched at it again and again, and when I had made up a good deal of fire-dust, I emptied it into the handful of dry brown grass in my other hand intending to carry it home and keep it always and play with it. But the wind struck it and it sprayed up and spat out at me fiercely. I dropped it and I ran. When I looked back, the blue spirit was towering up and stretching and rolling away like a cloud, and instantly I thought of the name of it—SMOKE!—though, upon my word, I had never heard of smoke before.

Soon brilliant yellow and red flares shot up through the smoke, and I named them in an instant—FLAMES—and I was right, too, though these were the very first flames that had ever been in the world. They climbed the trees, then flashed splendidly in and out of the vast and increasing volume of tumbling smoke, and I had to clap my hands and laugh and dance in my rapture, it was so new and strange and so wonderful and so beautiful!

He came running, and stopped and gazed, and said not a word for many minutes. Then he asked what it was. Ah, it was too bad that he should ask such a direct question. I had to answer it, of course, and I did. I said it was fire. If it annoyed him that I should know and he must ask, that was not my fault. I had no desire to annoy him. After a pause he asked:

"How did it come?"

Another direct question that also had to have a direct answer.

"I made it."

The fire was traveling farther and farther off. He went to the edge of the burned place and stood looking down, and said:

"What are these?"

"Fire-coals."

He picked up one to examine it, but changed his mind and put it down again. Then he went away. *Nothing* interests him.

But I was interested. There were ashes, gray and soft and delicate and pretty—I knew what they were at once. And the embers; I knew the embers, too. I found my apples and raked them out and was glad, for I am very young and my appetite is active. But I was disappointed—they were all burst open and spoiled. Spoiled apparently, but it was not so; they tasted better than raw ones. Fire is beautiful; some day it will be useful, I think.

ADAM. – She says the snake advises her to try the fruit of the tree, and says the result will be a great and fine and noble education. I told her there would be another result, too— it would introduce death into the world. That remark was a mistake—it would have been better to keep it to myself. It only gave her an idea—she could save the sick buzzard and furnish fresh meat to the despondent lions and tigers. I advised her to keep away from the tree. She said she wouldn't. I foresee trouble. Will emigrate.

EVE. – I saw him again, for a moment, at nightfall, but only for a moment. I was hoping he would praise me for trying to improve the estate, for I had meant well and had worked hard. But he was not pleased, and turned away and left me. He was also displeased on another account: I tried once more to persuade him to stop going over the Falls. That was because the fire had revealed to me a new passion—quite new, and distinctly different from love, grief, and those others which I had already discovered—FEAR. And it is horrible! I wish I had never discovered it. It gives me dark moments, it spoils my happiness, it makes me shiver and tremble and shudder. But I could not persuade him, for he has not discovered fear yet, and so he could not understand me.

ADAM. – I have had a variegated time. I escaped last week and rode a horse all night as fast as he could go, hoping to get clear of the Park and hide in some other country before the trouble should begin. But it was not to be. About an hour after sun-up, I was riding through a flowery plain where thousands of animals were grazing, slumbering, or playing with each other, according to their custom. All of a sudden they broke into a tempest of frightful noises, and in one moment the plain was a frantic commotion and every beast was destroying its neighbor.

I knew what it meant—Eve had eaten that fruit, and death was come into the world. The tigers ate my house, paying no attention when I ordered them to desist. They would have eaten me if I had stayed, which I didn't, but went away in much haste.

I found this place, outside the Park, and was fairly comfortable for a few days, but she has found me out. Found me out, and has named the place Tonawanda—says it *looks* like that. In fact I was not sorry she came, for there are but meager pickings here, and she brought some of those apples. I was obliged to eat them, I was so hungry. It was against my principles, but I find that principles have no real force except when one is well fed. She came curtained in boughs and bunches of leaves, and when I asked her what she meant by such nonsense, and snatched them away and threw them down, she tittered and blushed. I had never seen a person titter and blush before, and to me it seemed unbecoming and idiotic. She said I would soon know how it was myself.

This was correct. Hungry as I was, I laid down the apple half-eaten—certainly the best one I ever saw, considering the lateness of the season—and arrayed myself in the boughs and branches I had just taken away from her and discarded. Then I spoke to her with some severity and ordered her to go and get some more and not make a spectacle of herself. She did it, and after this we crept down to where the wild-beast battle had been. We collected some skins, and I made her patch together a couple of suits proper for public occasions. They are uncomfortable, it is true, but stylish, and that is the main point about clothes. Another thing—she says it is ordered that we work for our living hereafter. She will be useful. I will superintend.

After the Fall

ADAM – TEN DAYS LATER. – She accuses *me* of being the cause of our disaster! She says, with apparent sincerity and truth, that the Serpent assured her that the forbidden fruit was not apples, it was chestnuts. I said I was innocent, then, for I had not eaten any chestnuts. She said the Serpent informed her that "chestnut" was a figurative term meaning an aged and moldy joke. I turned pale when I heard that, for I have made many jokes to pass the weary time, and some of them could have been of that sort, though I had honestly supposed that they were new when I made them. She asked me if I had made one just at the time of the catastrophe. I was obliged to admit that I had made one to myself, though not aloud. It was this. I was thinking about the Falls, and I said to myself, "How wonderful it is to see that vast body of water tumble down there!" Then in an instant a bright thought flashed into my head, and I let it fly, saying, "It would be a deal more wonderful to see it tumble *up* there!"—and I was just about to kill myself with laughing at it when all nature broke loose in war and death, and I had to flee for my life. "There," she said, with triumph, "that is just it; the Serpent mentioned that very jest, and called it the First Chestnut, and said it was coincident with creation and had caused the fall." Alas, I am indeed to blame. Would that I were not witty; oh, that I had never had that radiant thought!

EVE.– When I look back, the Garden is a dream to me. It was beautiful, surpassingly beautiful, enchantingly beautiful. And now it is lost, and I shall not see it any more. The Garden is lost, but I have found him, and am content.

ADAM. – I find she is a good deal of a companion. I see I should be lonesome and depressed without her, now that I have lost my property.

EVE. – He loves me as well as he can; I love him with all the strength of my passionate nature, and this, I think, is proper to my youth and sex. If I ask myself why I love him, I find I do not know.

It is not on account of his gracious and considerate ways and his delicacy that I love him. No, he has lacks in this regard. But he is well enough just so, and is improving.

It is not on account of his ambition that I love him. I think he has it in him, and I do not know why he conceals it from me. It is my only pain. Otherwise he is frank and open with me—now. It grieves me to think that he would keep a secret from me, and sometimes it spoils my sleep thinking that he must have some secret ambition, but I will put it out of my mind—it shall not trouble my happiness, which is otherwise full to overflowing.

And it is not on account of his brightness that I love him. No, it is not that. He is not to blame for his brightness, such as it is, for he did not make it himself. He is as God made him, and that is sufficient. In time his brightness will develop, though I think it will not be sudden. And besides, there is no hurry; he is well enough just as he is.

It is not on account of his education that I love him. He is self-educated, and he does really know a multitude of things, even if they are not so.

It is not on account of his chivalry that I love him—no, definitely not that. He told God on me about the apple thing, but I do not blame him. It is a peculiarity of his sex, I think, and he did not make his sex. Of course I would never have told on him. I would have perished before doing that, but that is a peculiarity of my sex. I can't take credit for it, for I did not make my sex.

I suppose the kind of love I feel for him is not a product of reasoning and statistics, like one's love for other reptiles and animals. I think this must be so. I love certain birds because of their song; but I do not love Adam on account of his singing. His singing sours the milk, and the more he sings the less I get reconciled to it. Yet I ask him to sing because I wish to learn to like everything he is interested in. I know it will be hard to ever like this particular thing, but I will try.

Then why is it that I love him? At bottom he is good, and I love him for that. But I could love him even were he not so good. He is strong and handsome, and I love him for that, and I admire him and am proud of him.

But I could love him without those qualities. If he were plain, I should love him anyway, and if he were a wreck, I should love him all the same. And I would work with him and would pray for him and stay by his side until I died.

So I think I love him merely because he is mine and is masculine. There are no other reasons, I suppose. This kind of love is not a product of reasonings and statistics. It just *comes*—none knows from where—and it cannot explain itself, and doesn't need to. This is what I think. But I am yet only a girl, the first that has examined this matter, and it may turn out that, in my ignorance and inexperience, I have not got it right.

ADAM – NEXT YEAR. – We have named it Cain. She caught it while I was up country trapping on the North Shore of the Erie. She caught it in the timber a couple of miles from our dug-out—or it might have been four, miles, she isn't certain which. It resembles us in some ways and may be a relation. That is what she thinks. But in my judgment this is an error. The difference in size warrants the conclusion that it is a different and new kind of animal.

EVE. – At first I didn't understand what was happening to me, but God gave me abundant intuition, so I figured it out. Adam didn't notice I was changing, that my belly was slowly growing. He didn't even notice when my belly had grown to the point where it resembled a watermelon. I thought by then he would notice and would ask me if I had swallowed a seed. I thought that he'd want to thump my belly to judge what my property had produced. I tried hinting about what was really happening to me, what was happening to us, but he didn't catch on. And since he does not take well to being told anything that he thinks he already knows, which is just about everything, I decided to keep my secret.

So after it arrived, I told him I found it. I kept my secret and will keep it until he figures it out himself, though a mystery remains for me as well. For how this event all played out from start to finish, I am not so sure myself.

ADAM. – Perhaps it is a fish. When I put it in the water to find out, it sank, and then she plunged in the water and snatched it out before I could decide the matter. I still think it is a fish, but she is indifferent about what it is and will not let me have it again to try to find out. I do not understand this. The coming of the creature seems to have changed her whole nature and made her unreasonable about experiments.

EVE. – Just so long as he stops experimenting with our creature and does not do it any harm, I will let him solve the mystery by himself. He feels so proud when he figures things out, and I will be sure to admire him when he does.

ADAM. – She thinks more of this animal than she does of any of the others, but she is not able to explain why. Her mind is disordered—everything shows it. Sometimes she carries the fish in her arms half the night when it complains. At such times the water comes out of the places in her face that she looks out of, and she pats the fish on the back and makes soft sounds with her mouth to soothe it. She betrays sorrow and attentiveness in a hundred ways. I have never seen her do like this with any other fish, and it troubles me greatly. She used to carry the young tigers around so, and play with them, before we lost our property. But it was only play; she never took on about them like this when their dinner disagreed with them.

EVE. – When he decided he liked me, he began to act like he wanted me all to himself. The moment I knew what had happened to me, I feared that he would not want to share me with another one of our kind. When he finally does find out the truth, I still fear he will not want to keep it or will never want to have any others. Maybe I do not give him enough credit. I will be patient. He may learn to like it when he becomes accustomed to it. How could he not?

ADAM. – She doesn't work on Sundays, but lies around all tired out, and likes to have the fish wallow over her. She makes fool noises to amuse it and pretends to chew its paws, and that makes it laugh. I have not seen a fish before that could laugh.

ADAM. – It isn't a fish. I cannot quite make out what it is. It makes curious devilish noises when not satisfied, and says "goo-goo" when it is. It is not one of us, for it doesn't walk. It is not a bird, for it doesn't fly. It is not a frog, for it doesn't hop. It is not a snake, for it doesn't slither. I feel sure it is not a fish, though I cannot get a chance to find out whether it can swim or not. It merely lies around, and mostly on its back, with its feet up. I have not seen any other animal do that before. I said I believed it was an enigma, but she only admired the word without understanding it. In my judgment it is either an enigma or some kind of a bug. If it dies, I will take it apart and see what its arrangements are. I never had a thing perplex me so.

EVE. – Did I determine his 'brightness' was sufficient before continuing to consider what it was that might explain why I love him? Good grief! Did he say it might be a bug? Did he really say that?

ADAM – THREE MONTHS LATER. – The perplexity increases. I sleep but little. It has ceased from lying around, and goes about on its four legs now. Yet it differs from the other four legged animals because its front legs are unusually short. Consequently this causes the main part of its person to stick up uncomfortably high in the air, and this is not attractive.

It is built much as we are, but its method of traveling shows that it is not of our breed. The short front legs and long hind ones indicate that it is of the kangaroo family. But it is a marked variation of that species since the true kangaroo hops whereas this one never does.

Eve reconciles it by persuasion, and by giving it things which she had previously told me she wouldn't give it. As already observed, I was not at home when it first came, and she told me she found it in the woods.

It seems odd that it should be the only one, yet it must be so. I have worn myself out these many weeks trying to find another one to add to my collection, and for this to play with; for surely then it would be quieter and we could tame it more easily. But I find none, nor any sign of any.

EVE. – Honestly! He is not even getting warm! And yet—thank goodness—he is beginning to warm up to it. He even wants to find another one like it for the sake of it. Isn't that sweet? I have hoped from the beginning that someday he will come to love it as I do. Now I think there is a chance that he will.

ADAM – THREE MONTHS LATER. – The Kangaroo still continues to grow, which is very strange and perplexing. I never knew one to be so long getting its growth. It has fur on its head now. Not like kangaroo fur, but exactly like our hair except that it is much finer and softer. And instead of being black, it is red. If I could catch another one—but that is hopeless. It is a new variety, and the only sample; this is plain. But I caught a true kangaroo and brought it in, thinking that this one, being lonesome, would rather have that for company than have no kin at all, or any animal it could feel a nearness to or get sympathy from in its forlorn condition here among strangers who do not know its ways or habits, or what to do to make it feel that it is among friends. But the kangaroo was a mistake—it went into such fits at the sight of the kangaroo that I was convinced it had never seen one before. I pity the poor noisy little animal, but there is nothing I can do to make it happy. If I could tame it—but that is out of the question. The more I try the worse I seem to make it. It grieves me to the heart to see it in its little storms of sorrow and passion. I wanted to let it go, but she wouldn't hear of it. That seemed cruel and not like her, and yet she may be right. It might be lonelier than ever; for since I cannot find another one, how could it find one?

EVE. – He is trying my patience. I should have told him long ago what it is and what it will be. He said he is eliminating possibilities through the process of deduction. But there is an entire animal kingdom of possibilities, and he seems intent on considering everything before he hits upon the obvious. How many clues and hints does he need before he figures this out? He is missing the forest for the trees. I like that phrase. I shall use it when I drop another hint.

ADAM – FIVE MONTHS LATER. – It is not a kangaroo. No, for it supports itself by holding to her finger, and thus goes a few steps on its hind legs, and then falls down. It is probably some kind of a bear and yet it has no tail—as yet—and no fur, except upon its head. It still keeps on growing. That is a curious circumstance, for bears get their growth earlier than this. Bears are dangerous since our catastrophe—and I shall not be satisfied to have this one prowling about the place much longer without a muzzle on. I have offered to get Eve a kangaroo if she would let this one go, but it did no good—she is determined to run us into all sorts of foolish risks, I think. She was not like this before she lost her mind.

ADAM – A FORTNIGHT LATER. – I examined its mouth. There is no danger yet: it has only one tooth. It has no tail yet. It makes more noise now than it ever did before—and mainly at night. I have moved out. But I shall go over, mornings, to breakfast, and see if it has more teeth. If it gets a mouthful of teeth it will be time for it to go, tail or no tail, for a bear does not need a tail in order to be dangerous.

ADAM – FOUR MONTHS LATER. – I have been off hunting and fishing a month. Meantime the bear has learned to paddle around all by itself on its hind legs, and says "poppa" and "momma." It is certainly a new species. This resemblance to words may be purely accidental, of course, and may have no purpose or meaning. But even in that case it is still extraordinary, and is a thing which no other bear can do. This imitation of speech, taken together with general absence of fur and entire absence of tail, sufficiently indicates that this is a new kind of bear. The further study of it will be exceedingly interesting. Meantime I will go off on a far expedition among the forests of the north and make an exhaustive search. There must certainly be another one somewhere, and this one will be less dangerous when it has company of its own species. I will go straightway; but I will muzzle this one first.

EVE. – Muzzle? That'll be the day. I do not worry about keeping our first one safe and secure anymore as I am well into the process of perfecting what I need to do in every situation to get my way. But I am concerned about the future. Must I spend a lifetime with him pointing out things that are as obvious as a huge, bulging belly? This is the second time that he hasn't noticed such an obvious thing about me. That irritates me. That really irritates me.

ADAM – THREE MONTHS LATER. – It has been a weary, weary hunt, yet I have had no success. In the meantime, without stirring from the home estate, Eve has caught another one! I never saw such luck. I might have hunted these woods a hundred years, I never would have run across that thing.

ADAM – NEXT DAY. – I have been comparing the new one with the old one, and it is perfectly plain that they are of the same breed. I was going to stuff one of them for my collection, but she is prejudiced against it for some reason or other, so I have given up the idea, though I think it is a mistake. It would be an irreparable loss to science if they should get away. The old one is tamer than it used to be and can laugh and talk like a parrot, having learned this, no doubt, from being with the parrot so much. I shall be astonished if it turns out to be a new kind of parrot. And yet I ought not to be astonished, for it has already been everything else it could think of since those first days when it was a fish. The new one is as ugly as the old one was at first. It has the same sulphur-and-raw-meat complexion and the same singular head without any fur on it. She calls it Abel.

ADAM – TEN YEARS LATER. – They are Boys. We found it out long ago. It was their coming in that small immature shape that puzzled us—we were not used to it.

EVE. – Perhaps I overdid the 'we' thing. He uses it incorrectly all the time now. But I will gladly suffer his mistakes. Perhaps I was made for that. I am used to it and comfortable with it.

ADAM – FIVE YEARS LATER. – There are some girls now. Abel is a good boy, but if Cain had stayed a bear, it would have improved him.

Reflections

ADAM. – After all these years, I see that I was mistaken about Eve in the beginning; it is better to live outside the Garden with her than inside it without her. At first I thought she talked too much; but now I should be sorry to have that voice fall silent and pass out of my life. Blessed be the chestnut that brought us near together and taught me to know the goodness of her heart and the sweetness of her spirit!

EVE. – It is my prayer, it is my longing, that we may pass from this life together. It is an immortal longing—it shall never perish from the earth. It shall have place in the heart of every wife that loves until the end of time; and it shall be called by my name. But if one of us must go first, it is my prayer that it shall be me. Perhaps I am being selfish—I fear he would not manage well without me. But life without him would not be life; how could I endure it? This prayer is also immortal, and will not cease from being offered up while my race continues. I am the first wife; and in the last wife I shall be repeated.

At Eve's Grave

ADAM. – Wheresoever she was, THERE was Eden.

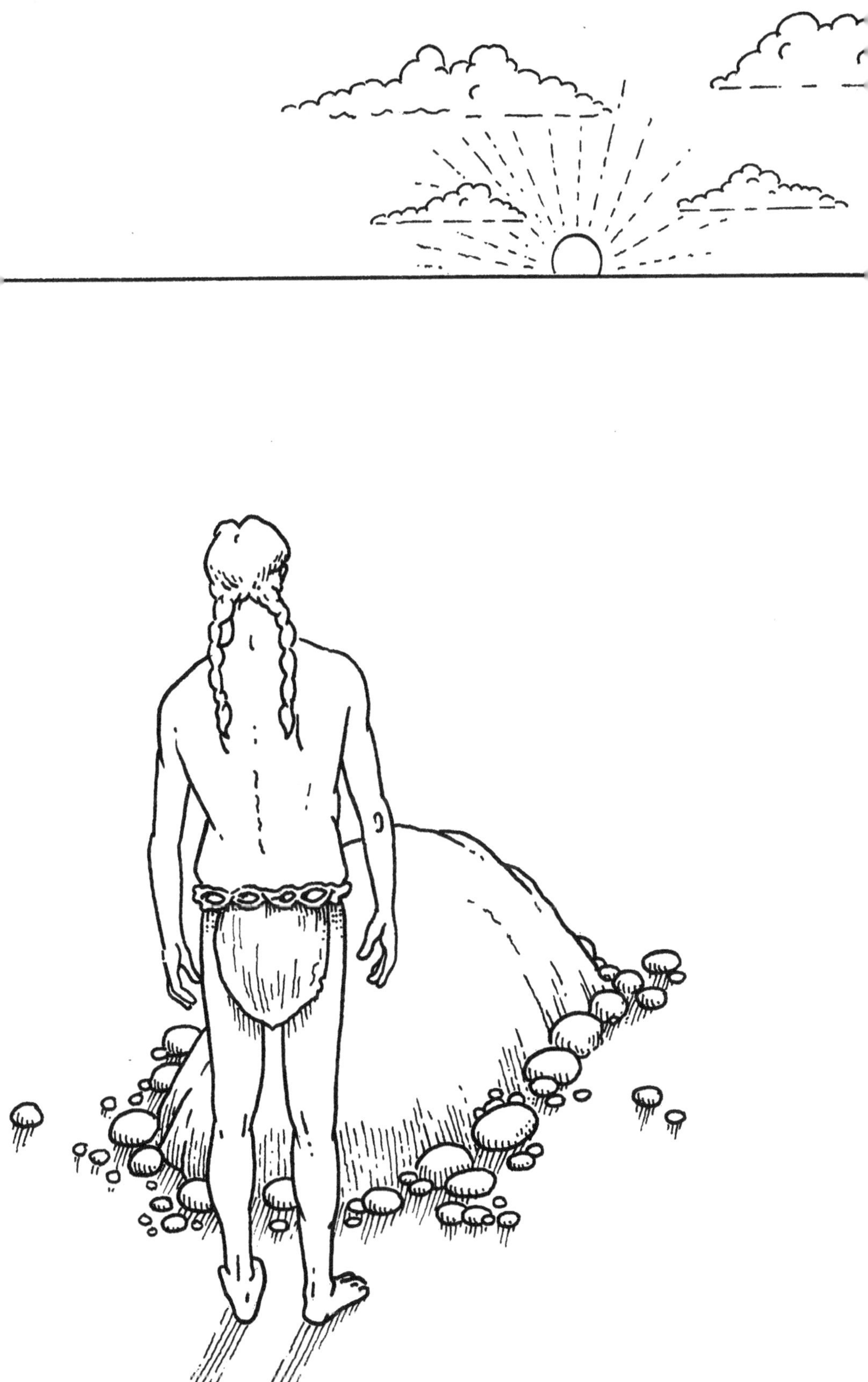

EVE & ADAM

Mark Twain was the greatest humorist of his time—most would say of all time. But he was always more than a humorist. Even before the height of his success and fame as a humorist, Mark Twain was an 'idea' man, and that never changed. He was as interested in challenging people to think as he was in making them laugh. Sometimes he slipped challenging ideas about human nature into humorous stories on the sly. At other times, as in his landmark and justly revered Adventures of Huckleberry Finn, Twain presented challenging ideas straight up and on the surface.

As he advanced in age, and after experiencing deeply personal losses and hardships, Mark Twain's humor turned darker and his attitude and ideas more cynical. Near the end of his life he wrote a series of six stories commonly known as the 'Adamic Diaries'. Four of the stories poke fun at Christianity and are dark in tone. These stories were not published until after Twain died in 1910. Two of the six stories in the series were published as illustrated books while Twain lived—Extracts from Adam's Diary in 1904 and Eve's Diary in 1906. These two stories are less pointed and much lighter in tone. We intertwined them in this volume by rearranging text and adding a little new material.

Contrary to Twain's wishes, the stories were not published in one volume until after his death. Considering them separately, Eve's Dairy is primarily a tender and loving story. It is thought to be Twain's eulogy to his deceased wife, Olivia. Extracts from Adam's Diary goes mainly for laughs. While Twain depicts Adam to be love-resistant at first, he nevertheless, and cleverly, sets the couple's location within creation at Niagara Falls, the honeymoon capital of the world. The stories work well apart, but even better when read consecutively (or we think, when blended as in this volume). Taken together, the two stories put Eve's and Adam's sometimes sweet, sometimes humorous views of creation more effectively at odds.

Twain was often taken to task for his ideas and his willingness to poke fun at people and institutions. After the publication of Eve's Diary, an article in a newspaper criticized Twain for falsifying the bible story of creation by making Eve the namer of things and creatures. Twain responded by saying story-tellers are independent of facts and privileged to rearrange them to meet the requirements of the situation. He said that when he was hot with the fires of production, he would even distort the facts of the multiplication table, let alone the facts of Genesis.

MARK TWAIN
(1835-1910)

Mark Twain was born in Florida, Missouri on November 30,1835 and raised in Hannibal, Missouri, a small town on the Mississippi River. But that's not exactly true. For Mark Twain's legal name was Samuel Clemens, and he was always just plain Sam to family and friends. Mark Twain didn't exist until 1863 when Sam adopted this pen-name while working as a newspaper reporter in Nevada. Soon Mark Twain, author, was writing humorous stories and thought-pieces for readers across the nation. Meanwhile, Mark Twain, lecturer, was cracking-up audiences with finely-polished stories, delivered to perfection. Blessed with remarkable talent for both written and oral story-telling, talents he cultivated with diligent practice, Mark Twain became a famous author and lecturer almost all at once. It didn't take long before Mark Twain's fame spread internationally nor before it became permanent as gold with the publication of *Adventures of Huckleberry Finn* in 1884.

Mark Twain spoke and wrote in a quaint, authentic American dialect with pride and self-assurance at a time when almost all authors thought they needed to stick with high-tone English to earn respect and acclaim. Yet there was something even more crucial to Mark Twain's fame than his innovative literary style; he perfected a method to make people laugh. A serious man at heart, Mark Twain took serious subjects and situations and exaggerated them to a point where potential drama turned into hilarious comedy. His perfection of this comic method caused tears of laughter to wet the cheeks of countless listeners and readers in his day, as it has for generations of readers ever since. Mark Twain became and remains an international treasure mostly because he was so darn funny.

After a long and abundant career, Mark Twain succumbed to heart disease and died in Redding, Connecticut on April 21, 1910. Many millions of fans world-wide mourned his death.

The *Adapted Classics* Collection

Contemporary classic illustrations in *Adapted Classics* books add expression to visually-rich stories by world-famous authors. Lightly modified and illustrated to suit and attract modern young readers, stories in the *Adapted Classics* collection are respectful renditions of timeless stories from the world of classic literature.

View the entire collection at: www.adaptedclassics.com

Marc Johnson-Pencook is an illustrator, animator, and muralist. He lives in Minneapolis, Minnesota. His illustrations appear in books, periodicals, gallery shows and private collections, and his murals adorn many walls and ceilings in public places and private spaces in the Twin Cities and beyond. He also teaches illustration at the Atelier Studio Program of Fine Art in Minneapolis and the Art Academy in St. Paul. In addition, Marc composes and performs rock music—he currently plays percussion for Mod Gods of Nod—a psychedelic rock band based in Minneapolis. Marc can be contacted at: http://illustratormarc.com/

Jerome Tiller lives in Minneapolis, Minnesota. He is owner of ArtWrite Productions, a publishing company bent on making education and reading more pleasurable for youth. Adapted Classics, an imprint of ArtWrite Productions, uses fine-art illustrations to introduce classic stories to young readers. Learn more about Jerome and his company at: artwriteproductions.com and adaptedclassics.com

IF YOU LIKE THIS STORY, PLEASE LET OTHERS KNOW IN WHATEVER WAY(S) YOU CHOOSE.

www.ingramcontent.com/pod-product-compliance
Lightning Source LLC
Chambersburg PA
CBHW040545170726
48295CB00012B/598
* 9 7 8 1 9 3 9 8 4 6 3 4 1 *